# Behind the Cop Mask

a short story compilation

Annie Kool

# DEDICATION

To my children, always

# CONTENTS

The Trailer Park............................................1

Moment Captured.......................................8

Angels Lead...............................................22

The Assault Within.......................................28

Angels in the Snow.....................................37

Author's Biography....................................46

BEHIND THE COP MASK

# The Trailer Park

I'd slipped into the driver's seat before it hit me. It was as though the music had stopped and in its place, silence marched.

The rain had already started, the sky angry in its grayness.

I turned the key in the ignition and felt the familiar roar of the engine come to life. Familiar because I'd driven the same make and model time after time. But that was in training.

I glanced in the rearview mirror toward the building. I spotted the man I was looking for. My trainer, smoking his cigarette by the back door. Thankfully.

I needed time. Time to savor this first real moment of being a cop.

I needed to wrap myself around the moment for as long as it would allow. I wanted to explore my thoughts and the sensations surrounding them.

I wondered how I should be feeling at this moment. Filled with self-importance I now had a badge? Yet, instead, I found I was humbled with a tremendous task. A task that would require me to make instant and life-altering decisions, decisions that would impact not only myself but those around me.

A sharp tap interrupted my thoughts on the window. I turned to see my trainer, with the butt of his flashlight against the window. I opened it, just enough to hear his voice but not enough to allow the plunging wetness to engulf me.

My trainer smiled and opened the door. "Get out. I'm driving". I crinkled my nose at him but quickly gathered myself out of the driver's seat and obligingly turned it over. I raced to the passenger's door, not wishing for the rain to settle onto my carefully starched and creased uniform.

We logged our call signs into the computer and wheeled out of the parking lot. Other police officers were either testing their emergency equipment or strapping their duty bags into the passenger's seat, while others were pulling out of the lot. Our duty bags were in the trunk. The back seat reserved for the unknowns.

I settled in for the ride, the rain and the wiper blades hypnotic in their consistency. I wondered what the night would bring us, besides the inevitable rain. And then the calls came in, the dispatcher non-relenting. And they didn't stop. Not just for us, but for every car on the street.

Every call was worthy of a book. Every call was disturbing, and every call was exciting and my adrenaline was reborn. I thought about how I would need to journal and to remember all the pains of humankind. And yet I did not. I could not.

Over the years, the calls ran into one, and they no longer seemed as exciting, and they no longer were deemed noteworthy.

But there was that one call that first night, I will always remember.

The icy rain plunged mercilessly from the skies that night, drowning one's thoughts in its relentless attempts to wash away the miseries of what would unfold.

It must have been three or four AM and it was black out, wet, eerie. Perhaps eerie because I wasn't from a place where the rains never stopped. Not like this. Or perhaps only eerie because I wasn't used to any of this.

The call came in. A female caller. From a phone. A pay phone. A phone that was in a ballpark.

There was a man with a gun, and he was going to kill her. And we flew. We flew over the roads until we hydroplaned in our need to reach her. And then we were there. At the phone, at the edge of a ball field. And the rains didn't stop. And the receiver.

It just swung, to and fro in the dark, alone, between sheets of rain.

There was no one. She was gone.

Our lights flashed through the field in a vain attempt to fight through the rain and the darkness.

Nothing. And then we saw it, across the street. In the deathly quiet of the night, with no sound but that of the rain pouring, the lights of an old car running in the trailer park.

We drove up to the car and stopped at a safe distance. A distance of thirty feet; maybe forty. Another rookie and their trainer pulled in beside us. Our lights on the old car.

The driver's door opened. We saw legs. Two of them. Our doors opened. Four of them. We got out. We used our doors as a shelter from what was to come. A sea of rain, or perhaps of bullets.

We yelled out, "Police! Get out of the car, show us your hands!" and there was no response.

Just movement. Slow movement.

We yelled again, our guns out of our holsters. Pointed at the man with the legs in the old car. And we yelled, and we yelled and there was no response.

Then slowly, ever so slowly, a man immersed from the depths of the old car.

Slowly, painfully, and he wouldn't listen. And as he stood, one arm was draped with newspapers with something black in his hand and the other arm, his left one was behind his back. He inched forward.

All we knew was we had a gun call and there was no one else awake or around and the rain that wouldn't stop. That is what we knew.

And we knew that this man had one arm concealed under newspapers with something black in his hand and the other one behind his back. And we knew that he was walking towards us, slowly. Ever so slowly. And we knew that as loud as we yelled and demanded that he show his hands that he wouldn't. And that more deliberately than words could explain, he marched steadily, painstakingly, towards us.

His right arm, under the papers with the black thing in his hand, whatever it was. The other concealed behind his back. And that grin on his face. He came forward to us and time stood still.

We demanded, we shouted. "Police! Show us your hands! Drop it! Put your hands up." All in vain. Our shouting couldn't stop what was happening, what was about to happen.

And then my trainer moved away from the shelter of the driver's door and began walking, slowly, towards the old man with the grin, the black thing in his hand, newspapers draped over his arm and the other arm, nowhere, behind his back.

I stayed behind the passenger door, using it as a coat of armor between myself and the man. I glanced quickly at the other car and noticed the other two police officers had their own guns drawn and pointed still.

I recall wondering what my trainer was doing and if he was insane.

I remember my finger on the frame of my gun, and I was locked into a stare at the man and his arm that was nowhere behind his back.

I knew, without a doubt, if his arm came forward, my bullet would stop him in his tracks and his finger would never pull that trigger. I was ready, my gun aimed at his center and I stood there, sure of what I needed to do, and I knew the others were doing the same.

And as suddenly as it began, it was over. My trainer was there, standing in front of the man. It was only when it was over that my blood began to pump again, hard, to make up for lost time, the time it had stood still. My heart was left pounding in my chest and I breathed, again.

The man wasn't dead, he hadn't tried to kill us and in his hand, draped in newspapers was a flashlight. He took so long coming out of the car because he was manipulating newspapers in such a way as to drape them over his arm, there, in the trailer park. And the reason his other arm stayed behind his back? It wasn't there. It was amputated at the elbow. And the reason he didn't hear us was because he was hard of hearing and suffered from the beginnings of dementia. And the grin? He was just so happy to see us, the police, in the middle of the night, in the rain.

That was my night, my first night, the night we could have killed a man. A man, delivering newspapers, on a dark and rainy night. And I thought we would not have deserved to live if we had killed him, and I realized how close and how bad it could have been.

I felt deep-seated shame and yet there was no need. It was only by the grace of God things hadn't gone wrong.

I was too new, and it rocked me to my core. And although we did what we had to do, what we were called to do, I couldn't help but feel silenced and humbled at the power our decisions and actions held, not just for ourselves but for our country and the people we served.

~ The End ~

# A Moment Captured

The chill of the morgue engulfed me.

Cold on steel swallowed me. The clasps snapped open on my briefcase, echoes in the stillness, the morgue quiet, as it should be.

I checked my watch. I'd timed it well, enough time to set up for the autopsy and to review the file before the team of pathologists and investigators arrived.

Reaching for the file folder, I leaned against the wall. Her photo, stapled to the front of the file. I looked at the date. Five days ago, on Santa's knee, at the local mall. I checked her birthdate, three years old. Three years old and dead.

Looking back at me was the picture of an angel, her

eyes the color of the Atlantic, blue, dark and deep, her excitement shining through the camera. Her hair, styled in loose blond ringlets, bounced in unison, stilled momentarily for the camera.

She'd worn a dress, velvet and lace, Christmas red. Her shoes, black patent, one tucked behind the other as she perched gingerly, bravely and smiling in all of her three-year-old glory, there on Santa's knee. Tights so woolly and white, itchy, I thought. A candy cane held tightly in her tiny, sticky fist. A moment captured, frozen, for this, her last photo.

I thought of the mother who would have bathed her and dressed her that morning, the mother who would have had to urge her little girl to stay clean for Santa. I wondered if they had ice cream later or if maybe hot chocolate and marshmallows were more appropriate for this time of year. Or perhaps the little girl hadn't even liked hot chocolate. I wondered if she had held that candy cane tightly in her little fist for the rest of that day.

And I wondered at how her mother could find the courage to bury her baby this Christmas: to place her little body into the frozen, hard ground. My heart ached for her, knowing that the anguish would be far more than anyone could bear. I marveled at the human heart and its capacity of all that it must endure. I prayed silently for this mother as I blinked back a tear and wondered if she could even stand today.

I thought of the little girl and anguished for the life she would never live and I thought of the medical team and the investigative team and how difficult today would be for each of us and how we would somehow carry this child and her mother in our hearts for a lifetime. There wasn't a heart cold or calloused enough that wouldn't. We would carry them forever.

Tragedies were like that, it didn't matter if they were old or young; we carried them. But the young, we carried longer and larger, sometimes too large, their lost lives shifting and sifting and at last settling in some way into our lives. And I was thankful for that; that our humanness remained, despite the cost.

For some, the cost was too high and everyone managed to find a cross to carry, to hoist to their already burdened shoulders and many never laid their burdens down.

Through the years, the use of numbing, in whatever form that might take, was there. For some it was alcohol, for others it was drugs. For others, it was sex, and for others it was shopping. For others, it was taking out their rage on their loved ones. And equally wrong, there were those who shut out the world around them, closing themselves from friends and family, the possibility of life and love. And yet, for others, the addiction to adrenaline seeking was their demise.

Very few who faced endless tragedies walked away unscathed. We replaced laughter with sarcasm, hope for cynicism.

Christmas was but days away. I thought of my own children at home. In their pajamas and slippers, watching cartoons and eating their cereal between excited longing at the tree and the presents found there. I had little gifts I still needed to pick up and others I would still need to wrap.

The thoughts of all the things I had to do, between the foods I had to shop for, prepare and cook, the cleaning I would need to do and yet, I was here. Doing what I needed to do, what I was called to do. Searching for answers for a child who would not celebrate her Christmas and for her mother whose presents for the little girl would remain unopened.

I wanted nothing more than to be home with my own children, making them stacks of pancakes for breakfast, maybe with little ears and a little smiling face made with raisins. Yet, I couldn't and I knew that.

I just hoped that somehow in their child-like minds they understood why I had to go over and over again.

I wondered too how they could really understand, when they couldn't be a part of the life's anguish that I had to deal with, the stories that unfolded for me, not ones for their little ears or hearts. They were often more than even I could bear.

I hadn't brought my children to see Santa this year, somehow too busy or too exhausted to make the effort. I thought of how I needed to make the time because we truly had time; we weren't corpses like the others in this tomb of cold and quiet death.

I tore myself away from my own world, turning again to the task at hand. The little girl's file folder.

Her medical history was unremarkable. She was a healthy and beautiful child, who was now gone. I flipped the pages to the investigational reports. I hadn't been there to attend the scene.

First responders had attended a typical run-down nineteen seventies apartment building after receiving a 911 call from the little girl's mother.

The mother had found her baby, unresponsive, stiff and cold to her touch. She had been sleeping on the couch with her, the little girl tucked on the inside so she wouldn't roll to the floor.

Her little face was found stuffed into the cushioned folds of the back of the couch.

She was dead. Had been for hours, judging by the stiffness of her body and the cold of her skin.

I wouldn't have time to review the entire file. I needed to prepare the morgue; bring her body to the stainless-steel dissection table, ready the equipment for her autopsy. It was something I did, in addition to my extensive caseload; I found a sense of comfort in preparing the morgue for the team. It grounded me, helped me to focus on the life lost, as though I found it too evasive to simply march in on someone's corpse, watch it be opened and study a piece of a person they themselves had never seen.

I needed that quiet time to reflect, to know a part of them.

I smiled at myself; full well knowing that it was my way of coping with the endless human suffering and anguish that work threw my way, a self-protection, and an inward and silent cry for peace, for understanding. Of this, I was sure. And if I could ground myself by the methodical preparation of the workspace, then that's what I needed to do.

I wondered at the dead I had encountered throughout the years. So often you left feeling better for having met them, even though it was in the coldness and loneliness of death. The stories their loved ones would tell me, or the belongings I rifled through, their poetry, their love letters, their journals, so rich, so painful, so beautiful.

Sometimes there was so much to learn, and sometimes there was so little. And at other times, when I examined every angle I could of someone's life, there on paper and through different lenses of their being from different friends and loved ones, I felt as though I knew them on a different level than anyone else could have, their lives exposed. And I'd walk away wishing that I had met them in life.

The sad ones were those who died alone, old and cold, the only confirmation of their death a foul odor detected by a stranger, the mailman or the neighbor passing by. And as you searched through what they left behind, to discover who they were, you found nothing but an emptiness and loneliness that consumed their souls and all that they clung too.

What message did they leave behind? Even their families, when you at last located them, did not wish for a service or even an obituary and at the worst, refused to claim the body and the state would take responsibility.

There are a million lonely and wounded souls out there, and at times I was awestruck at the inability to find anyone who might have loved them or whom they might have loved. Certainly, there was someone or were they so wounded they simply closed the door, life more than they wished to entertain.

This little girl wouldn't be one of them, but what little child could be or should be?

I opened the door of the cooler; there were only seven stretchers. And every body filled the stretcher except hers. And you could tell without reading the tags, without unzipping the bags, that she was the one against the wall. The tiniest one, the wrong one, the one that screamed it shouldn't be there.

I wondered at how many years it might take for me to open that cooler door and not flinch.

I smiled at myself, thinking about how professional I appeared from the outside. My feet already wrapped in morgue slippers, my body clothed in scrubs, my latex gloves in place. My hair covered. My insides screaming, telling me I should work in a coffee shop or a bookstore and to stop doing this to myself. But I was born for this, I knew this too. And because of this, I wouldn't and couldn't ever stop.

I moved the stretchers around until I could squeeze hers through the cooler doors and towards the stainless-steel table that would be used for her autopsy. The table was too cold, too sterile for anyone to end up there, and yet she had, and it was our job to find out why.

I unzipped the bag, the plastic stiff from the cold. And there she was, the same little angel from the picture, and she looked like a doll, unmoving, her eyes fixed and now awkward in her face. And but for the lividity on the left side of her face, unscathed.

I searched her eyes for petechiae, asphyxiation, but why? What would stop a three-year-old from moving her little face away, even in sleep, when suffocating?

What had stopped her from turning her face away from the back of the couch, even if the couch had been bulky and overstuffed? It didn't make sense, couldn't make sense. And yet, was foul play even considered or had this been a case of neglect. But even with neglect, how was it that she was unable to move her face to gasp for the air she needed?

It was too soon to consider the answers, the autopsy would provide its own findings and conclusions, the toxicology samples and the investigators evidence of the scene would need to be examined first but my restless and questioning mind sprang ahead, wanting the answer before it was time.

She was wearing a nightgown, what should have been white with pink edging, a faded silhouette of Cinderella on the front. The nightgown itself grayed and pilled; uncared for. The remains of what may have been spaghetti and ketchup on her sleeve.

Her blonde curls matted about her face, as though she had perspired on her way to death. I touched her curls with my gloved hand and swept them away from the sides of her face. Such a beautiful child now stilled.

The pathologist arrived, along with the team of

investigators, their usual banter silenced. We worked quietly, each of us far too cognizant of our own little ones at home and far too aware how swiftly death could come.

Completing an autopsy on a little girl isn't something anyone should have to do, have to witness. Yet there we were and oddly enough there was nowhere else I could imagine being. We had to know. We needed the answers.

The first cuts were the worst, the cutting of her ribs the most painful. So different from the adult ribs we were accustomed too. They were as dewy as springtime willows, so incredibly pliable under the bone cutters.

Her tiny organs weighed, sliced and examined. Samples placed in jars for microscopic examination. And we watched as the pathologist worked on, speaking his findings into his voice recorder for the stenographer to decipher. Assisting where and when we could.

The skin was carefully sliced from the back of one ear

to the other. Her skin, then torn away from her scalp, flapped over her face. Her casket would be open and it was important to ensure that those who loved her did not see that an autopsy had been completed, the grief already far too great.

I forced myself from being human, the tearing away of her skin from her skull bone, just the sound of it, I couldn't do it anymore, couldn't take it, and I looked at the guys around me and knew that they couldn't either, but each of us continued, the task at hand greater than our need to scream and yell, that this couldn't be real.

Everything was weighed and sliced and dissected and examined.

Our results were inconclusive. She was dead; she had suffocated in the back of the couch while she slept there with her mother, but the question remained, why.

Toxicology samples were taken, blood urine and vitreous fluid. Her eyes, sunken now, emptied. And we closed her up again, her stomach contents emptied, her heart and liver and kidneys weighed and measured, sliced for examination, samples retained. And we sewed the gaping cavity closed, placing all of her organs within her tiny little body before doing so.

We gently placed her back into the body bag, ready for the funeral home. Our autopsy was inconclusive and with the toxicology tests, hopefully we would still find an answer.

The investigators showed the photographs they had snapped at the scene. The apartment outdated, unkempt. They knew the family, knew the father of the little girl and said that he was in jail.

The mother was on social assistance, and when they arrived she had just woken from a night of partying. Four men were sleeping on the floor, throughout the debris of what the little girl would have called home.

The photograph of the fridge showed a fridge without food, except for some mayonnaise. There was alcohol in there, though. Not much.

It had been a wild night. Or so it appeared in the photographs. One investigator said that he thought death was perhaps the easiest thing the little girl would have had to face in her life.

There were empty beer bottles in every photograph. There was an empty vodka bottle; several emptied pop bottles and even more bottles of emptied rum.

I felt sick, wanting to stop what I was hearing, seeing.

The mother had smelled of alcohol and cigarettes that morning. She had broken down and wept and been unable to stop. She had been so drunk the night before that she barely remembered passing out on the couch.

She vaguely remembered her little girl coming to her in the night with her little arms outstretched and how she had lifted her little body over hers and placed her, snuggled by her side, on the inside of the couch so she would not fall to the floor in her sleep. And instead she had died.

Her mother thought she had come to her at five that morning, but wasn't sure. She only knew she had woken hours later, to find her daughter cold and stiff beside her and that she had been to blame, for whatever had taken her baby from her and that her little girl's head was stuffed into the back of the couch.

She had called 911, and she had woken the drunken men up off the floor. And they didn't remember the little girl from the night before, not if she had been there, not if she had eaten with them, nor if she was up at all during the night.

All they knew was they had been drinking endlessly and woken up on the floor to a hysterical mother whose baby was dead.

They had provided their statements to the police. And they were sick about it. They had partied too much.

And that was all.

There was nothing else that they could say nor offer to help with because they simply didn't know. And the police and the paramedics and the firefighters had stood there and done what they needed to do, each of them anguished at the scene that enfolded before them.

It wasn't unlike the little girl to rise up at night and walk through the apartment to find her mother. And it wasn't unlike that girl child to wake up to a mother who was too drunk to hear her cries for something to drink. And it wasn't unlike that little girl to wake up to different men sleeping on the floor that she would have to crawl over to find her mother. And it wasn't unlike that little girl to pull that big fridge door open with her tiny arms and find nothing at all to drink there.

In the end, it wasn't too difficult to understand that the thirsty little girl would walk amongst the passed out partiers to find bottles with leftover beer or other alcohol and to lift them to her mouth.

When the toxicology reports were completed, the results found her blood alcohol content was so high it was a miracle she was able to stumble to her mother, to raise her little arms and say 'up' and to be lifted to her final moments, there beside her drunk and wasted mother.

The little girl; drunk and wasted herself.

We stood there in silence. Our pain too deep for words, our hearts broken. And we thought of the family, the grandparents, the mother, the father, the uncles and aunts, and we were shaken to our core.

This little life was now gone. And we knew then why she had been unable to lift her little angelic face from the seat and the back of the couch. She was drunk, completely and totally drunk, and she wouldn't have known. And her mother was drunk, completely and totally drunk, and she wouldn't have known. And now she was gone.

As we gathered her things, and called the funeral home to have her body removed from the morgue, we went through the paper bag of belongings her mother had brought in for her.

Inside were the clothes she was to be buried in, the ones that everyone would see when they would say their final goodbyes to her in her tiny casket; the Christmas dress with the white lace, the black patent little shoes and the white tights.

I remembered my briefcase and the candy cane that my own little girl had plucked off the tree for me that morning and said "For your work, Mommy."

I glanced around and noticed that everyone was too busy writing in their notebooks to notice me. I went to my briefcase and found the little candy cane tucked in the side. I placed it in the pocket of her little Christmas dress and whispered, "God bless you little one."

A silent tear trickled out of the corner of my eye as I quietly left the coldness and sorrow of the morgue.

~ The End ~

# Angels Lead

Dawn was touching the edges of the night's sky.

It was over. I glanced at the clock on the dashboard. Four thirty. Just enough time to fill the empty tank, toss the old coffee cups and make it back to Headquarters.

I was exhausted. Another seemingly endless night, filled with the usual. I couldn't wait to get home, slip out of my uniform and crawl into bed. Hopefully I'd be asleep before the sun began piercing my inadequate blinds, telling my body that there was nothing normal about sleeping the day away. I'd had enough.

Enough or not, the calls didn't stop; the dispatcher's voice unrelenting, summoning another police car for yet another call.

"Twenty-three alpha seventeen, we have a noise complaint at Main, called in by a male advising that his crackhead brother had been yelling earlier and now wouldn't turn the TV down. The male caller lives in the attached garage, while the brother lived in the basement suite of his eighty-four year old mother's house. Could I get another car to back up twenty-three alpha seventeen?"

I reached for my radio. "Twenty-three bravo-twenty en-route." I clicked on my computer screen to locate the address; tapped on the GPS map system and was on my way. It was an easy call and I still had a few minutes before the shift was over.

I guided the car through the now quiet city streets.

Bainbridge was already there as I crept up the street. I

liked Mike. He was a solid guy and a smart cop. Even better, he was a fair cop. He knew how to handle people. Regardless of whom they were or what they had done. He was good to them, but never soft. And I respected him for it.

I could see him; see that he was speaking to a male on the sidewalk in front of a house. He spotted me and walked over.

"That's the guy who called. Guess he's something pissed, hasn't slept. Claims his brother is a crackhead and a heroin junkie. He heard his brother yelling at two this morning. Figures he was yelling at his mother. He heard his brother say 'give me some fucking money'. Looks like he went out for a bit after that and now he's got the TV just cranked."

I looked at my watch, it was five now. The call had originally come in at two. We'd been too busy to attend to a simple noise complaint.

Bainbridge rolled his eyes. "Go figure, these guys are both in their fifties and live with their mother. Jesus, what's with that?"

I shrugged. "Life I guess."

He went on, "Anyway, buddy lives in a suite separate from the house. His crackhead brother lives in the house with mom but spends most of his time in the basement. He goes to the basement door and tells his brother to turn the shit down. Brother tells him to go fuck himself and locks the door; turns it even louder."

"Let's go tell him to knock that shit off so people can sleep." I suggested.

We picked our way through the darkness to the basement door. Mike pounded on it, "Police, open up!"

The television was cranked. We both pounded. "What do you want?" came a voice from within. We both spoke up, "Open the door!"

We heard a click of a dead bolt opening. "Open the door"!

"Let yourselves in." the voice chimed back.

We opened the door. Nostrils assaulted with the stench of crack and dirty ashtrays. He was seated on the couch, the television blaring over the stench.

"What's going on tonight? What's with the loud TV?" Mike asked.

"Sorry officers, I'll turn it off. Was just going to bed."

"What are you doing up at five in the morning with the television cranked?" I questioned.

"I was just waiting to do my paper route."

He sat at the edge of his couch, leaning forward. It didn't feel right.

I asked him, "Who lives here with you?"

He said his Mom did.

"Where is she?" I asked.

"Sleeping." he nodded upwards.

I looked at Mike. "I'm going to see her." Her name was Lena, he said.

Angels led.

I started past the man, past the couch and up the stairs, the long dark stairs to the upper level. There was a door at the top of the stairs. I opened it quietly and asked myself what I was doing. It wasn't right to search a residence for a simple noise complaint.

I walked through the darkness. Feeling my way down a hallway. "Lena," I called quietly, "Lena."

I walked past several closed doors to the end of the

hall. I could hear a gurgling sound. I thought, why am I here, what am I doing? This poor old lady has a cold and is sleeping soundly. I shouldn't be here, I shouldn't wake her, I will scare her to death.

Yet, the angels led.

"Lena, it's the police." I whispered. "I'm going to turn on the light okay? I want to talk to you."

The gurgling was disturbing. I thought she must be really sick. I turned on the light. And my heart stopped.

There was blood all over the bed. False teeth knocked out of her mouth, her ear, torn from her head, hanging, lifeless. Her neck; a battlefield of bruising. Unconscious. I roused her.

"Lena, Lena!" I cried to myself and to her. And I thanked the angels that led me there.

I grabbed my radio, "Arrest him for aggravated assault.

Please." I rolled her over and she came to. Dark blood gurgled from her chest and out of her mouth.

Her neck was already black from a chokehold. I realized that her lungs had been full of blood and that she must have been lying there for hours. And it broke me.

I knew that there was no reason for me to have gone upstairs to find her. And I knew that something had led me to her. And I knew without a doubt that she was grasping for her last breaths. And I knew I was Angel led.

By the time the ambulance arrived, the bedroom was a crime scene. The son was on his way to jail and the forensic unit had arrived.

I went to the hospital then. The doctors had said I had saved her, she had been drowning in her own blood and if I hadn't found her, she surely would have died.

I breathed again with the full realization that angels led.

There was no reason for me to have gone upstairs. It wasn't I who had saved her, I'd only walked where angels tread.

~ The End ~

# The Assault Within

Would it have mattered in the end, if you or I had gone forward, pursued what was right? Or was it best left undone; your feared flight of scorn, a path untraveled?

I still remember the pain in your eyes when you told me.

When you showed me your lip, swollen and bloodied, broken and bruised with humiliation. And when you removed your tie and undid your buttons, pulling aside your uniform to reveal your breast, fingerprints of blues and greens, the rage of humanity. And how I was left silent, across from you, there at the local diner.

Our friendship strong in the early dawn with the sun fluttering and beckoning rays of warmth as the anger seeped like molten lava through me.

I'd asked you breathless, what happened.

I wondered how I could feel so incredibly helpless, unable to will my blood to continue its endless journey throughout my body, unable to lift my coffee to my lips.

Everything stood still.

I knew that you would tell me, you'd come this far and I knew as a cop, I wasn't going to let it go, whatever it was. But I also sensed you were unsure, what to say, how to say it and what I would do with it, because you too were a cop.

I looked at you then, my eyes begging you to tell me. You said I couldn't tell anyone. That I needed to promise you at least that.

My head nodded, knowing I needed to agree for her to tell me but also fully aware I might, if I had to, whatever it was. Those bruises of fingerprints a blood war of violence in my mind.

You and I were beat cops, nothing else. We had to work hard on the streets and sometimes we had to fight even harder. It was a tough town, a mean town.

We carried our firearms snug at our hips, our other weapons within reach on our belts and we were strong. As strong as a woman could be. Yet, I wondered if we were strong enough for this, for whatever it was that had happened to you, because now it was personal, and we both knew it.

In the end, I don't think we were, or that we embraced our strength as we should have. To this day, I am filled with anguish that your pain had no release. I wonder if now that we no longer speak, if somehow you've found some peace. I haven't. Not yet.

"Tell me." I urged you. Tell me.

You nodded and the threat of tears sought your eyes and you blinked at them, your dark eyes broken.

Tell me. And you did.

It was out on the Flats you'd said.

My mind shifted to the endless nights in the heat of the valley. Where the ground was dust and every step provoked a brown cool mist of sifted icing sugar.

I pictured the Flats, the clapboard shacks of the area and I nodded, still confused.

You had been doing scene security for a murder, a body that was dumped. I remembered that. I'd been there too. For a bit. You had stayed the night with one of the guys to do scene security.

The body belonged to a young man, lifeless and covered in tattoos. Executed, and dumped with all the markings of a gang slaying. They'd said he was from the city.

They'd found him off the main road, down a dry and dusty trail, dragged there, meant to be found.

My mind felt blanched, exhausted.

You gave me more details then.

You were there with one of the new guys, just out of training. Scheduled to sit there from seven at night until seven in the morning when the homicide detectives could arrive and work in the daylight hours.

I barely knew him, I had nodded to him at Headquarters. You told me you and the new guy had sat there for a few hours, in the police cruiser. The music low, the engine running and the headlights casting light across the crime scene.

His name was Jerry. I asked you if he was a nice guy and I still didn't know. Otherwise I wouldn't have asked you that. Not until you told me he had out of nowhere grabbed you in the passenger's seat and began forcing his mouth onto yours, grabbing at your breast and pulling it hard against him.

Groping at your crotch through your pants and biting your lip open; how you fought him off of you and asked him what the fuck he was thinking as you sat there, trembling and crying in your rawness, hurt and confused.

You looked at me then and asked me how he could have done that, he was a cop and you didn't know what you had done to make him do that to you. And I said you hadn't done anything. And you cried, the tears winning now, pouring down your face and past your broken lip. You were so confused. You didn't understand why he attacked you.

You blamed yourself for what happened. And I thought how could you blame yourself? But I knew, it was because you were a girl, even though you were a cop, even though you knew better.

You'd blame yourself, somehow, someway because it must have been something that you had done. And even though you'd told a hundred girls over the years it wasn't their fault, and never could be, you didn't and couldn't believe that in yourself.

I held you then as you sobbed into me.

I said that I couldn't ignore the information, because what he had done was completely and totally unforgivable. I'd said I would ensure he was charged and lost his badge.

As a police officer I refused to have someone like that on the police force. It didn't matter that I wasn't the chief. No one would stand for that. Not inside the police force and not outside of it.

You railed against me, furious, horrified you had trusted me and that you obviously in the end could not.

You had not told a soul but me because you thought you could trust me and you had needed to tell me because there was no one else.

I asked you why the hell you would tell me shit like that if you expected me to not say a word. How you expected me to allow a piece of shit like that to work on the streets and how if he would do that to you, another cop, what would he do to the girls on the streets?

You said you knew, that he couldn't be on the streets and that you feared for others, yet you begged and begged for me not to say a word and I was adamant.

Adamant that I couldn't not say a word, that my very lifeblood and work demanded I do something.

You begged me to wait a few days.

I asked you what you were afraid of and you said you were afraid that somehow you would be the one everyone would look down on. That everyone would say you had lied and had come on to him. You thought he would turn it all on you and say he was targeted. You said he would lose his job and you didn't want to be responsible for that.

I was saddened you felt this inappropriate responsibility for what might happen to his job. His behavior was his choice, not yours.

You said you were terrified none of the guys would ever want to work with you again. I firmly disagreed. I told you there wasn't a guy in the police force who would think of it that way; you had been sexually assaulted by another cop and it was cut and dried. But you begged, and pleaded and cried for me to wait, to give you a few days.

I cried at your loss and now my loss because we were at a crossroads. I instinctively knew, our friendship had changed for ever. That inevitably you would shut me out, and you did. My friend, my incredible friend, how did this happen, how could this happen?

The calls came in and we had to go. The day was endless, consumed with all the pains of human kind and I didn't get to talk to you again that day.

It didn't help that I needed to go to the city for training for a few weeks the next day. I lost sight of you, and I couldn't reach you. And maybe if I was there, I could have changed your mind, but I wasn't.

You called me a few days later. Crying and angry, threatening our friendship and my reputation, arguing with me for hours that if I did go forward you would deny the story, change it, make me appear as a liar.

I realized I couldn't fight it. That if you denied it and if Jerry denied it there was no crime. It would be my word against both of yours and I would be the one that would be criticized, despised and rejected. That's the way it worked in the police force and I was well aware of it. I'd wear the label of a rat.

You didn't know I was tormented for you, that I couldn't sleep for days and that I didn't know where to turn.

I couldn't ask another police officer for guidance because then they too would be dragged into the sickness of this tale and tormented too, for you.

I remembered too the time I did go forward with something that was horrendous and how that officer was hauled into the Staff Sergeant's office in front of me and my partner and asked, "Did you do this?" and how he denied it, right there, and how we left, feeling the fool for it.

Me and my partner, our mouths wide open. We were so horrified we never spoke of it again. It took all of our courage to go forward, days of struggling with the wisdom of it all, and we ended up looking like fools. I didn't want that again, and I knew how easily it could happen, in a world where things were best left unsaid and where the 'whistleblower' was far too often shunned, no matter what it was they had seen.

Heartbroken, I called a friend in Texas. Someone who knew the streets better than I, someone who understood the system inside and out but also someone who wasn't involved, a different police department, who could stand back and tell me what to do.

I told him about you. I told him everything and he said I needed to step back, do as you wanted, because in the end, if you denied the attack, denied you were a victim, there wasn't a crime.

He was as horrified as I was, sickened you didn't want to move forward, lay an official complaint and have Jerry charged.

The kid didn't deserve a badge, much less to be walking on the street, a free man.

I knew that no matter what I did, or how I attempted to present it; if you wouldn't tell them what happened; no one could do anything to help you in the end.

Jerry would be free to walk the streets, a cop,
someone respected and with authority.

I had to leave it, and walk away from it.

I struggle with what he has done since and to whom,
and I wonder if you do too. I wonder if he's hurt
someone else and if your decision has haunted you.

Was there a reason you chose to protect this man and
his undeserved badge?

~ The End ~

# Angels in the Snow

The restaurant is empty with the exception of the
regulars. There is nowhere else to go. It's always the
old men and us.

My hands are frozen, I said. Silence.

"Cold out there." Idle chatter I knew it was too late
for.

Everyone just wanted to go home.

My hands wrapped around the mug of coffee.
Exhausted, I wondered if I had wanted the coffee or
just the warmth it might offer.

The day would break soon enough and I would be
released to the warmth of my unmade bed and the

troubled sleep of those who have seen too much.

I gazed through the reflection of the window to the parking lot outside. The snow was falling again, cold and whirling.

Christmas was a week away. I still had time to make it special, if I even cared enough to try. Night shifts did that to me. The exhaustion carried me into a fog, oblivious to the seasons and the march of days.

I thought of our small town, nestled in the arms of the mountains, swathed in snow, and the people that lived there.

I thought of those curled up in their warm beds, safe from the bitterness that made up the night. The terror we'd seen on the streets was something they would hopefully never know or even imagine.

I remembered the homeless, curled up outside the old Mission, hunkered in the doorways with frayed and filthy discarded shreds of what someone in a better place once called a blanket.

If they were lucky, if lucky was the word.

Others found cardboard, first wet then frozen,
offering what warmth they could, huddled between
the dumpsters.

The buildings lined the alley, at times a shelter from
the wind and at other, crueler times, a funnel, racking
cold across stiffened bodies.

I thought of their hands, cracked and blackened.
Nicotine stained and crack pipe scorched, scalded
from the flames. I wondered if the burning somehow
felt right at the time, against the cold. I shivered.

Our radios crackled and there was dispatch. False
hopes shattered there would be no more calls, that
our radios would remain silent.

The three old men shook their heads at us, in what by
now was an understanding. They were there every

night.

I wondered if they were old cops. Retired now, their sleep patterns still broken through the seasons of their lives and somehow addicted to the cold of the night, sleep a vague memory from their long ago youth.

I said I'd take it. It was late. Everyone else could return to the office to tackle their paperwork and get home to bed.

There was a vehicle down an embankment. Seventy miles northeast of town; I knew the area. No one else did. I grew up here, no one else did.

There was no cellular phone reception there and the caller didn't know if there was anyone in the car. Said he just noted tracks and dim headlights down an embankment. Said he called when he was back in service.

I buttoned up my parka. The volunteer firefighters

from the nearby village were on their way. The ambulance too.

I thought of hell as I walked out the door. My mind exhausted and playing games. If hell was frozen.

I nodded to the guys, "See you tonight." They offered to come, I told them not to worry, to get home on time and to at least try to get some sleep.

Christmas was coming after all.

Snow had already caked my windshield. I started the car and groped around on the floor for the wooden handle of the snow scraper. I already thought that I was crazy to head out there alone on these roads. But that was my job. It was simply crazy.

A job where you rushed in while everyone else rushed out.

I glanced into the windows of the restaurant; the guys were still sitting there, nursing cold hands around warm mugs.

I brushed the snow off the windows and from my headlights. Shivering, I crawled in behind the wheel of ice.

The snow squeaked beneath my tires. I cranked the wheel, the tires grinding themselves onto the empty highway, leaving the warmth of the café far behind.

The nearest village's firefighters and ambulance were there already. I could see the red flashing lights before I turned the corner.

It was cold. The snow was whirling, piercing my exhausted eyes.

I looked down the embankment. The car was right side up. It seemed far away. The lights were dimming, the battery exhausted. Judging by the snowfall on the tracks, as it careened over the cliff, it had been there for hours.

In the end, we knew they left the party early and between the snow storm and the drinks they'd had, the odds were against them. By the time we reached them it had been hours.

A firefighter showed me brain matter on the old electrical pole. They must have hit it hard before the car plunged down the embankment. They told me one of the girls was dead.

I slid down the embankment. Snow filling my boots and sliding up my jacket. The roof of the car was mostly ripped off revealing the girls. They couldn't have been much older than twenty.

Snow was piling on them, their hair, and their laps. If they were alive they'd be frozen. Their bare legs, their party dresses too thin. No coats. Their blonde hair, their magnificent curls. It must have taken hours to get ready and I thought how much fun they would have had. Their makeup still perfect, Barbies in the snow.

The driver was dead. Her body was cold; frozen in death. The girl in the passenger seat was alive. Barely. We got her out.

There was something strange about youth and beauty rolled into this death and this moment. There was something so haunting about this; a beautiful party, a deserted winter wonderland, and no one anticipating the horror the night would hold.

If it hadn't been for the tracks going off the road, who knows how long before anyone would have noticed. This haunts me; those thin party dresses and their perfect hair and the snow settling gently on their cold bodies.

And as I stood there, sickened by a life lost and another perhaps too, I peered into the back of the car and my heart stopped when I saw it. An infant's car seat. And I thought there was no way there was a baby, somewhere in the snow because there was no way these young ladies would have taken a baby to a party.

And then I thought, what if they had? What if the baby was lost in the snow? What if they hadn't been able to get a babysitter, what if this was the reason they left the party early to go home, to get the baby to bed? And I thought, was this the baby who no longer had a mom and as these thoughts rushed through me, tired and cold, my heart raced in my chest.

The snow was so deep and the night was so dark and yet, I plunged through it, through the trees, searching in quiet desperation.

The ambulance had gone. The girl, whisked away in the leftovers of a cold and bitter night, to be resuscitated, to breathe life into her frozen yet living body.

I called out to the firefighters, begging them to come, to help me. And they did. But they said, there is no baby. I called the Department Commander and begged him to wake the dog man, to come and help. And he said, there is no baby. There is no need. I said

there was, that we couldn't just think it was okay.
Because we didn't know for sure, nothing was ever
sure.

Fervently, I plunged and sank and moved through the
snow, through the trees at the bottom of the
embankment.

It was then I saw him.

A baby, in a dark blue snowsuit.

Thrown from the car, his arms and fingers
outstretched, as though surprised at leaving the
warmth of the car and to find himself hurtling
through the cold of the December night.

Those wings didn't carry him safely; instead they
brought him to eternal rest. His head twisted in ways
it shouldn't.

Instinctually I took off my parka and wrapped the
little baby in my arms and into its warmth, his body,

cold and stiff, his body that would no longer need the warmth. And I stood there, holding the little boy, and the tears washed over me and I couldn't will myself to carry him to the road.

The firefighters came and stood like fortresses around me, wrapping me into a coat and gently removing the baby from my arms as they led me, up the embankment. The embankment that had stolen so much.

They helped me into their truck to sit, to gather my strength, and to find warmth for my frozen hands and feet.

I urged them to go home, to get some rest, to allow healing to come after all they had seen and they left me then, alone, to wait for the traffic analyst and the coroner.

I wondered about the baby, why he had not been strapped into the car seat, and how the impact had sent him, hands outstretched through the night's cold air.

I mourned the little man he would have become but found some misplaced comfort that wherever his soul had gone, his mommy would be there too.

It struck me, how I had sat in the old cafe. My hands wrapped around a mug of steaming coffee and how cold I thought I was.

My thoughts turned to the girl who had lived and the hours she had lain in a car, in the bitter cold, her friend dead beside her; the snow gathering on their bodies as a baby lay alone dying in the snow and bitter cold.

She had survived and would survive and sadly so would her sorrow.

~ The End ~

**Author's Biography**

Annie Kool's debut release of a compilation of five short stories, explores the impact and heartache of policing on the front line. Her work as both a coroner and a police officer has provided her with an array of experiences. These experiences shine through in her fiction stories.

Annie lives with her cat and writes from her loft apartment. She is the proud mother of two grown children.

Annie can be reached at: Anniebkool@gmail.com

www.ingramcontent.com/pod-product-compliance
Lightning Source LLC
Chambersburg PA
CBHW071633140626
46555CB00022B/2742